Little Grey Rabbit's Christmas

Alison Uttley
pictures by Margaret Tempest

Collins

William Collins Sons & Co Ltd
London · Glasgow · Sydney · Auckland
Toronto · Johannesburg

First published 1939
© text The Alison Uttley Literary Property Trust 1986
© illustrations The Estate of Margaret Tempest 1986
© this arrangement William Collins Sons & Co Ltd 1986
Second impression 1987
Cover decoration by Fiona Owen
Decorated capital by Mary Cooper
Alison Uttley's original story has been abridged for this book.
Uttley, Alison
Little Grey Rabbit's Christmas. —
Rev.ed. — (Little Grey Rabbit books)
I. Title   II. Tempest, Margaret
III. Series
823'.912 [J] PZ7

ISBN 0-00-194211-5

Made and printed in Great Britain by
William Collins Sons and Co Ltd, Glasgow

FOREWORD

Of course you must understand that Grey Rabbit's home had no electric light or gas, and even the candles were made from pith of rushes dipped in wax from the wild bees' nests, which Squirrel found. Water there was in plenty, but it did not come from a tap. It flowed from a spring outside, which rose up from the ground and went to a brook. Grey Rabbit cooked on a fire, but it was a wood fire, there was no coal in that part of the country. Tea did not come from India, but from a little herb known very well to country people, who once dried it and used it in their cottage homes. Bread was baked from wheat ears, ground fine, and Hare and Grey Rabbit gleaned in the cornfields to get the wheat.

The doormats were plaited rushes, like country-made mats, and cushions were stuffed with wool gathered from the hedges where sheep pushed through the thorns. As for the looking-glass, Grey Rabbit found the glass, dropped from a lady's handbag, and Mole made a frame for it. Usually the animals gazed at themselves in the still pools as so many country children have done. The country ways of Grey Rabbit were the country ways known to the author.

I t had been snowing for hours. Hare stood in the garden of the little house at the end of the wood, watching the snowflakes tumbling down like white feathers from the grey sky.

"Whatever are you doing, Hare?" cried Squirrel, who sat close to the fire. "Come in! You'll catch cold."

"I am catching cold, and eating it too," replied Hare, happily.

"Hare! How long do you think Grey Rabbit will be? Can you see her coming? What is she doing?" called Squirrel again.

"She's at the market, buying Christmas fare for all of us," replied Hare, and he caught an extra large snowflake on his red tongue.

As he spoke, a small stout animal came trudging up the lane, laden with a heavy basket and a string bag bulging with knobs. Straggling behind was a little snow-covered creature.

"There she is!" cried Hare, leaping forward. "Make the tea, Squirrel."

He ran down the path, and then stopped, disappointed. "It's only Mrs Hedgehog!" he muttered. "And Fuzzypeg," he added, as he recognised the little fellow.

"Have you seen little Grey Rabbit?" asked Hare, as he leaned over the gate.

"I have indeed," said Mrs Hedgehog, resting her burden on the snow. "She was at the market along of me. Then she went to talk to Old Joe the Carpenter."

"What did she want with Joe?" asked Hare.

"Please Sir!" cried Fuzzypeg. "I knows, Sir. I knows what Grey Rabbit went to the Carpenter for."

"Sh-sh!" Mrs Hedgehog shook her head at her son. "You mustn't let the cat out of the bag." Then, picking up her basket, she continued on her way, with little Fuzzypeg protesting: "There wasn't a cat in the bag, Mother. There wasn't."

It was growing dark when Squirrel and Hare heard the sound of merry voices and the ringing of bells.

They ran to the door, and what should they see but a fine scarlet sledge drawn by two young rabbits, with little Grey Rabbit herself sitting cosily on the top!

"Oh Grey Rabbit, what a lovely sledge!" cried Squirrel, and she rubbed her paws over the smooth sides.

"Grey Rabbit! Our names are on it!" shouted Hare.

He pointed excitedly to the words, "Squirrel, Hare and little Grey Rabbit" written round the sides. "It's ours. It says so!"

"Yes. It is our very own," said Grey Rabbit. "I ordered it from Joe Carpenter, and these kind rabbits insisted on bringing me home."

After breakfast the next day, Squirrel and Grey Rabbit sat on the sledge, and Hare pulled them over the field.

They came to their favourite hill. Hare mounted behind them, and stretched out his long legs.

"One to be ready!

"Two to be steady!

"Three to be off!" he cried, and away they went down the steep slope.

"Whoo-oo-oo!" cried Hare. "What a speed! Whoops! Whoa!"

But the sledge wouldn't stop.

At last it struck a mole-hill, and over they all toppled, head over heels.

"Sixty miles an hour!" cried Hare, sitting up and rubbing his elbow.

Little Fuzzypeg, carrying a slice of bread and jam, came to watch the fun. He stared at the three dragging their sledge up the slope.

"I want to toboggan," he said softly, but nobody heard. "Look at *me* toboggan! Watch *me*!" cried Fuzzypeg. He made himself into a ball and rolled down the hill, faster and faster. When he got to the bottom there was no Fuzzypeg to be seen, only an enormous snowball.

"What a big snowball!" cried Squirrel, climbing off the sledge.

"What a beauty!" exclaimed Grey Rabbit.

"Help! Help!" squeaked a tiny voice. "Get me out!"

"What's that?" cried Squirrel.

"Help! Help!" piped Fuzzypeg.

"That's a talking snowball," said Hare. "Isn't that interesting? I shall take it home and keep it in the garden."

He dragged the large ball on to the sledge and pulled the load uphill. When he reached the top, Hare rolled the ball to the ground and gave it a kick.

"Ugh!" he cried, limping. "There's a thorn inside."

"Help! Help!" shrieked the tiny faraway voice. "Lemme out!"

"That's like Fuzzypeg's voice," said Grey Rabbit, and she bent over and loosened the caked snow.

Out came the little hedgehog, eating his bread and jam.

"However did you get inside a snowball?" asked Hare.

"I didn't get inside. It got round me," replied Fuzzypeg. "Can I go on your sledge now?"

Hare took the little hedgehog for a ride, but when Fuzzypeg flung his arms round Hare's waist, he sprang shrieking away.

"That's enough," he said. "My motto is, 'Never go hedging with a sledgehog'. I mean to say, 'Never go sledging with a hedgehog.'"

Fuzzypeg ran home and returned with a tea-tray. After him came a crowd of rabbits, each carrying a tray, and they all rode helter-skelter down the slope, shouting and laughing as they tried to race each other.

Squirrel, Hare and little Grey Rabbit took their sledge to Moldy Warp's house. Squirrel ran up the holly trees and gathered sprigs of the blazing red berries. Mole came out and showed them the mistletoe growing on an oak tree. And then he helped them to tie their branches on the sledge.

They said good-bye and hurried home.

Hare shut the sledge in the woodshed and carried the holly and mistletoe indoors. Grey Rabbit stood at the table making mince pies, and he and Squirrel decorated the room. They popped sprigs on the clock, over the corner cupboard, round the warming pan, and among the mugs on the dresser.

Little Grey Rabbit looked up from her patty-pans and waved her rolling pin to direct operations.

Up the lane came a little group, carrying rolls of music and pipes of straw. They talked softly as they walked up to the closed door of Grey Rabbit's house. They arranged themselves in a circle, they coughed and cleared their throats and held up their music to the moonlight.

"Now then, altogether!" cried an important-looking rabbit, playing a note on his straw pipe. "One, two, three!" and with their noses in the air they began to sing in small squeaky voices this Christmas carol.

"Holly red and mistletoe white,
The stars are shining with golden light,
Burning like candles this Holy Night.
Holly red and mistletoe white."

"Hush! What's that noise?" cried Hare, dropping his mistletoe.

"It's the Waits!" said Grey Rabbit, and she held up her wooden spoon.

They flung wide the door and saw the little group of rabbits and hedgehogs, peering at their sheets of music.

"Come in! Come in!" cried Grey Rabbit. "Come in and sing by the fireside. You look frozen with the cold."

"We're all right," said a big rabbit, "but a warm drink would wet our whistles."

Grey Rabbit took from the fire the two-handled Christmas mug of primrose wine, and the carollers passed it round.

Then they stood by the fire and sang all the songs they knew: "The Moon shines bright", "I saw three ships a-sailing", and "Green grows the holly."

"Now we must be off," they said, when Grey Rabbit had given them hot mince pies. "We have to sing at all the rabbit houses tonight. Good-night. Happy Christmas!"

Squirrel, Hare and little Grey Rabbit stood watching the Waits as they crossed the fields, listening to the carol, "Holly red and mistletoe white", which the animals sang as they trotted along.

"I think I shall take the sledge and toboggan down the hill by moonlight," said Hare.

He seized the cord of the sledge and ran across the fields to the hill.

Then down he swooped, flying like a bird.

Again and again he rushed down, his eyes on the lovely moon. Suddenly he noticed a dark shadow running alongside. It was his own shadow, but Hare saw the long ears of a strange monster.

"Oh dear! Oh dear! Who is that fellow racing by my side?" he cried.

He took to his heels and hurried home, leaving the sledge lying in the field.

"Did you come without the sledge?" asked Squirrel. "Hare, you are a coward! I don't believe there was anybody at all.

"You ran away from your shadow. You've lost our lovely sledge!"

"Better than losing my lovely life," retorted Hare. He felt rather miserable. "I suppose we had better go to bed," he muttered. "I don't suppose there will be any presents tomorrow. I don't think Santa Claus will find this house with so much snow about!"

He went upstairs gloomily, but he hung up his furry stocking all the same, and so did Squirrel.

When all was quiet Grey Rabbit slipped out of bed. Under her bed was a store of parcels. She opened them and filled the stockings with sugar-plums and lollipops. Then she ran downstairs to the kitchen, where the dying fire flickered softly.

31

She tied together little sprays of holly and made a round ball called a Kissing Bunch. Then she hung it from a hook in the ceiling.

On Christmas morning Grey Rabbit was so sleepy she didn't wake up till Hare burst into her room.

"Grey Rabbit! Merry Christmas! He's been! Wake up! He's been in the night!"

"Who?" cried Grey Rabbit.

"Santa Claus!" cried Hare. "Be quick! Come downstairs and see."

Grey Rabbit dressed hurriedly and entered the kitchen.

"Look at the Kissing Bunch!" said Hare. "Isn't it lovely! Let's all kiss under it."

So they gave their Christmas morning kisses under the round Christmas Bunch.

Robin the Postman flew to the door with some Christmas cards and a letter. The little bird rested and ate some breakfast while Hare examined the letter.

"It's from Mole," he said.

"Yes, I know," replied Robin. "Mole gave it to me."

"You're reading it upside down, Hare!" cried Squirrel. She took the little letter and read, "Come tonight. Love from Moldy Warp."

"It's a party!" cried Hare. "Quick, Grey Rabbit! Write and say we'll come."

Grey Rabbit sat at her desk and wrote on an ivy leaf, "Thank you dear Moldy Warp."

Then away flew Robin with the leaf in his bag.

All day they enjoyed themselves, playing Musical Chairs, pulling tiny crackers, crunching lollipops.

They all trooped to the hill to look for the sledge, but it wasn't there. Snow had covered all traces of footprints.

"Santa Claus has borrowed it," said Grey Rabbit. "When the snow melts we shall find it."

The first star appeared in the sky, and the three animals wrapped themselves up in warm clothes, and set off for Mole's house. They carried presents for the lonely Mole, and some of their own Christmas fare.

"What a pity you lost our sledge. We could have ridden on it tonight," said Squirrel to Hare.

When the three got near Mole's house they saw something glittering. A lighted tree grew by the path.

"Oh dear! Something's on fire!" cried Hare. "Let's put it out."

"Hush!" whispered Grey Rabbit. "It's a magical tree."

On every branch of the tree, candles wavered their tongues of flame. On the ground under the branches were bowls of hazel nuts, round loaves of bread, piles of cakes, small sacks of corn. There were jars of honey as big as thimbles, and bottles of heather ale.

"What do you think of my tree?" asked Moldy Warp, stepping out of the shadows.

"Is it a Fairy Tree?" asked Grey Rabbit.

"It's a Christmas Tree," replied Mole. "It's for
all the birds and beasts of the woods and fields.
Now sit quietly and watch."

Across the snowy fields padded little

creatures, all filled with curiosity to see the
glowing tree.

"Help yourselves," cried Mole, waving his
short arms. "It's Christmas. Eat and drink and
warm yourselves."

From behind a tree Rat sidled towards Grey Rabbit.

"Miss Grey Rabbit," said he. "I found a scarlet sledge in the field last night, and as your family name was on it, I took the liberty of bringing it here."

"Oh, thank you, kind Rat," cried Grey Rabbit, clapping her paws. "The sledge is found! Come Hare! Squirrel! Moldy Warp!"

The scarlet sledge was clean and bright and on the top was a fleecy shawl. From under it Grey Rabbit drew three objects. The first was a walking stick made of holly wood. The second was a little wooden spoon. The third was a wee bone box, and when Grey Rabbit opened the lid there was a little thimble inside which exactly fitted her.

"I've never had a thimble since Wise Owl swallowed mine," she said happily.

"Good Santa Claus," cried Hare. "He knew what we wanted."

"Only one person could make such delicate carvings," said Grey Rabbit.

"And that is Rat," said Squirrel.

"Three cheers for Rat!" cried Fuzzypeg, and they all cheered, "Hip! Hip! Hooray!"

Squirrel and Grey Rabbit climbed on the sledge, and Hare drew them over the snow.

"Good night. A happy Christmas!" they called.

"The same to you," answered Moldy Warp. The Hedgehog family waved and shouted, "Merry Christmas!"

"Heigh-ho! I'm sleepy," murmured Squirrel, "but it has been lovely. Thank you everyone for a happy day."

She curled down under the fleecy shawl by Grey Rabbit's side, clutching her wooden spoon. Grey Rabbit sat wide awake, her thimble was on her finger, her eyes shone with happiness.

Hare ran swiftly over the frozen snow, drawing the scarlet sledge towards the little house at the end of the wood.

Mistletoe white and holly red,
The day is over, we're off to bed,
Tired body and sleepy head,
Mistletoe white and holly red.